The Hides-It

Modern Curriculum Press
BEGINNING
TO
READ
Series

MODERN CURRICULUM PRESS
Cleveland • Toronto

The Hides-It

Judy Schoder

Illustrated by Dennis Hockerman

Library of Congress Cataloging in Publication Data

Schoder, Judith.
  The hides-it.

Summary: Sandy is amazed by the nighttime antics of his new toy.
(1. Toys—Fiction)   I. Title.
PZ7.S3648Hi   (E)   82-2367   AACR2

ISBN 0-8136-5123-9 (Hardbound)
ISBN 0-8136-5623-0 (Paperback)

    4 5 6 7 8 9 10   02 01 00 99 98 97

"Gramps, I'm home from the party!"
called Sandy as he ran into the
apartment. "Jeff's mom had us play a
game, and I won second prize."

5

6

"That's great, Sandy," said the boy's grandfather. "What was the prize?"

Sandy opened a bag and took out a little furry toy. It was part green and part pink. There were four curly horns on top of its head. And it had six tiny feet.

7

8

"I never saw a toy like that before," said Gramps. "What's it called?"

"A Hides-It," said Sandy. "I'm going to keep it on my dresser."

That night, before going to bed, Sandy placed the Hides-It on his dresser.

In the middle of the night, Sandy heard a strange sound in his room. He opened his eyes. Then he opened them wider. Sandy couldn't believe what he was seeing!

The Hides-It had jumped off the dresser. It had taken one of Sandy's shoes from under the bed and was dragging it across the room.

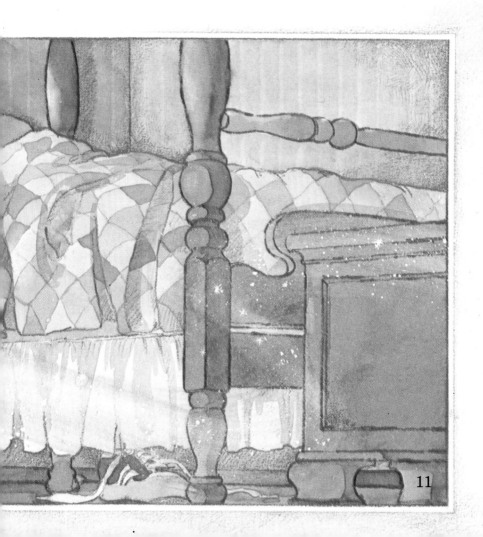

Sandy saw the Hides-It take the shoe into the closet. Then Sandy got out of bed. The closet door was open just enough for him to peek inside.

The Hides-It was hiding behind some boxes on the floor. With one pair of feet, it quickly pulled the shoelace out of Sandy's shoe. Then the Hides-It wrapped the lace around its four curly horns and tied the lace into a neat little bow.

13

14

The Hides-It began to laugh. It laughed and laughed until purple tears rolled down its round, furry body.

15

16

Then Sandy saw the Hides-It untie the shoelace from its horns. It started to put the lace back into Sandy's shoe.

17

Sandy crept back to his bed. He watched as the Hides-It put the shoe back under the bed and climbed up the dresser.

18

19

For a long time that night, Sandy couldn't sleep. He kept looking at the Hides-It. But the Hides-It didn't move. It didn't move at all. Finally Sandy fell off to sleep.

21

Early the next morning Sandy's grandfather came into Sandy's bedroom to wake him for school.

"Rise and shine," said Gramps. Then he patted Sandy gently on the head.

Sandy sat up in bed.

"Oh, Gramps," said Sandy. "The strangest thing happened last night."

Sandy told his grandfather about the Hides-It and what had happened in the closet.

"But, Sandy," Gramps said. "You know that toys can't jump off dressers or untie shoelaces. That was just a dream you had. A wild, crazy dream."

Sandy thought for a minute. "Maybe you're right, Gramps," said Sandy. "Maybe it was just a dream."

"Sure it was," said Gramps. "Now get ready for school. Your bus will be here soon."

Sandy ate his breakfast. Then he got washed and put on his clothes. Finally he went to get his shoes from under the bed. But one shoe was missing!

Sandy looked for his shoe in the closet. But it wasn't there. He looked all around the room. But the shoe wasn't in sight.

"Sandy, hurry," said Gramps. "Your bus is almost here."

Sandy went to the window to see if the bus had rounded the corner yet. When he pulled the curtain aside, his shoe fell off the windowsill. As Sandy picked up the shoe, his heart raced. The shoelace had been pulled out!

Sandy looked at the Hides-It on the dresser. The toy seemed to be smiling at him.

Then Sandy started to laugh. He was glad that he didn't win first prize at Jeff's party. First prize was an Eats-It. And if a Hides-It hides a shoe, then an Eats-It would probably eat it!

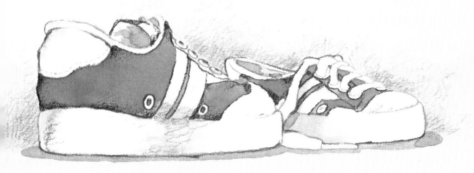

Judy Schoder is the author of many books and magazine articles for children and adults.

In addition to giving practice with words that most children will recognize, *The Hides-It* uses the 43 enrichment words listed below.

across	dragging	middle	second
almost	dream	morning	shoelace
apartment	dresser		started
aside		opened	strange
	enough		
bedroom		pair	thought
believe	finally	peek	
body	furry	placed	untie
breakfast		pulled	
	gently		windowsill
climbed	grandfather	quickly	wrapped
closet			
clothes	happened	rounded	
crazy	hiding		
crept			
curly	inside		
curtain			